Goatilocks
and the
Three Bears

Erica S. Perl *Illustrated by* Arthur Howard

Goatilocks
and the
Three Bears

SCHOLASTIC INC.

For Roo, who is a gem—E. S. P.

ISBN 978-0-545-82951-9

Text copyright © 2014 by Eric S. Perl. Illustrations copyright © 2014 by Arthur Howard. All rights reserved. Published by Scholastic Inc., 557 Broadway, New York, NY 10012, by arrangement with Beach Lane Books, an imprint of Simon & Schuster Children's Publishing Division. SCHOLASTIC and associated logos are trademarks and/or registered trademarks of Scholastic Inc.

12 11 10 9 8 7 6 5 4 3 2 1   15 16 17 18 19 20/0

Printed in the U.S.A.   40

First Scholastic printing, January 2015

Book design by Sonia Chaghatzbanian and Irene Metaxatos
The text for this book is set in Grit Primer.
The illustrations for this book are rendered in watercolor.

Once upon a time, there was a kid named Goatilocks.

She lived down the road from a family of bears.

When the bears went out
for a walk one morning . . .

well, you can probably guess what Goatilocks did.

Inside the bears' house, Goatilocks
found three bowls of porridge.

She tasted the big bowl,
but it was too hot.

She tasted the medium bowl,
but it was too cold.

Then she tasted
the little bowl. *Mmm!*
It was just right. So . . .

she ate it.

(The little spoon, too.)

Next, Goatilocks found three chairs.
She tried the big chair, but it was too hard.

She tried the medium chair, but it was too soft.

Then she tried the little chair.
Oooh! It was just right. So . . .

she ate it.

(Cushions and all.)

At this point, Goatilocks began to feel sleepy.
Upstairs, she found three beds.
She tested the big bed, but it was too lumpy.

She tested the medium bed,
but it was too squishy.

Then she tested the little bed.
Ahhh! It was just right. So . . .

she ate it.

(Plus the blanket,
two pillows,
and a pair of
pajamas.)

Then, with a contented sigh,
Goatilocks fell fast asleep.

Shortly thereafter, the bears came home.
You can probably imagine the commotion.

"Someone has been eating my porridge," said Papa Bear.

"Someone has been eating *my* porridge," said Mama Bear.

"Hey, where's my porridge?" asked Baby Bear.

"Get a load of this!" called Papa Bear from the dining room. "Someone has been sitting in my chair."

"Gracious!" said Mama Bear. "Someone has been sitting in *my* chair."

"Hey, where's my chair?" asked Baby Bear.

They found the culprit upstairs.
"My bed!" wailed Baby Bear. "It's . . . GONE!"
Goatilocks opened her eyes.

Above her stood three bears.

Quickly, she jumped up and hoofed it for home.
Which probably sounds like the end of the story.
But . . .

the next day, Goatilocks woke up
feeling a little, well, sheepish.
She wanted to make things right
with her neighbors. But how?

Outside, she found her answer.

How could the bears resist?
Her gift was so pretty.
So thoughtful.
It was just right.
So . . .

they ate it!